Marcus Pfister

THE RAINBOW FISH
EL PEZ ARCOÍRIS

North South   Edition bi·libri

Far, far away, in the open sea, lived a fish. But he wasn't a normal fish, no, no! He was the most beautiful fish in the entire ocean. His suit of scales sparkled in all the colors of the rainbow.

Lejos, muy lejos en alta mar vivía un pez. ¡Pero no era un pez cualquiera, no! Era el pez más hermoso de todo el océano. Su traje de escamas brillaba con todos los colores del arcoíris.

MARCUS PFISTER is the author of the phenomenally successful Rainbow Fish series, as well as many other books for children. He has worked as a graphic artist, a sculptor, a painter, and a photographer as well as a children's book creator.

North
South

Marcus Pfister was born in Bern, Switzerland. After studying at the Art School of Bern, he apprenticed as a graphic designer and worked in an advertising agency before becoming self-employed in 1984. His debut picture book, *The Sleepy Owl*, was published by NorthSouth in 1986, but his big breakthrough came 6 years later with *The Rainbow Fish*. Today, Marcus has illustrated over 50 books, which have been translated into more than 50 languages and received countless international awards. He lives with his wife Debora and his children in Bern.

for Brigitte

The Rainbow Fish by Marcus Pfister
© 1992 NordSüd Verlag AG, CH-8050 Zürich, Switzerland.
First published in Switzerland under the title *Der Regenbogenfisch*

This bilingual edition first published in 2019 by NorthSouth Books Inc., New York 10016
In association with Edition bi:libri, 80993 Munich, Germany.

English Translation © 2019 by Dr. Kristy Koth
Spanish Translation © 2019 by Dr. Olga Balboa Sánchez

Distributed in the United States by NorthSouth Books Inc., New York 10016.

The Library of Congress has cataloged the hardcover edition as follows: Library of Congress Cataloging-in-Publication Data
Pfister, Marcus.
[Regenbogenfisch. English]
The Rainbow Fish /Marcus Pfister
Translation of: Der Regenbogenfisch.
Summary: The most beautiful fish in the entire ocean discovers the real value of personal beauty and friendship.
[1. Beauty, Personal—Fiction. 2. Friendship—Fiction.
3. Fishes—Fiction.] I. Title.
PZ7.P448558Rai 1992 [E]—dc20 91-42158

A CIP catalogue record for this book is available from The British Library.

Printed in China, October 2020
ISBN: 978-0-7358-4371-4 (paperback edition)

3 5 7 9 11 · 12 10 8 6 4

Meet Marcus Pfister at www.marcuspfister.ch

FSC
www.fsc.org
MIX
Paper from
responsible sources
FSC® C007972

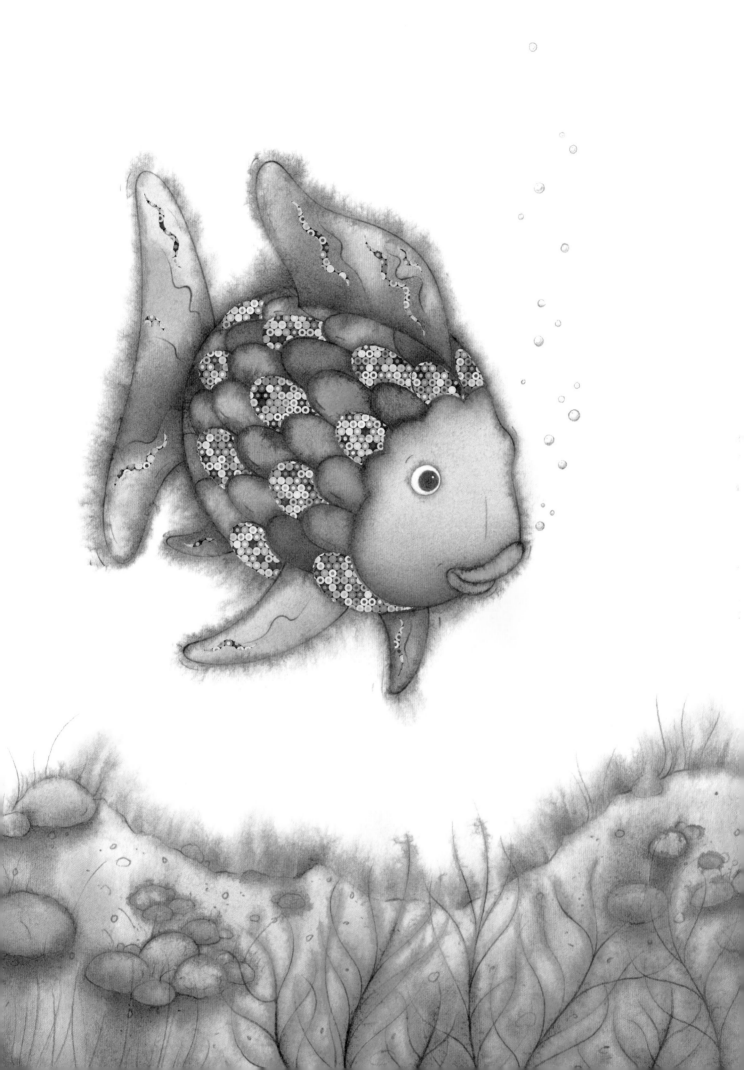

The other fish admired his colorful, sparkling suit of scales. They called him Rainbow Fish.
"Hey, Rainbow Fish! Come play with us!" But Rainbow Fish just glided past them, silent and proud, letting his scales glitter.

Los otros peces admiraban su brillante traje de escamas de colores. Y por eso lo llamaban pez Arcoíris.
"¡Hola, pez Arcoíris! ¡Ven a jugar con nosotros!". Pero el pez Arcoíris siempre se deslizaba callado y orgulloso a su lado mostrando sus escamas brillantes.

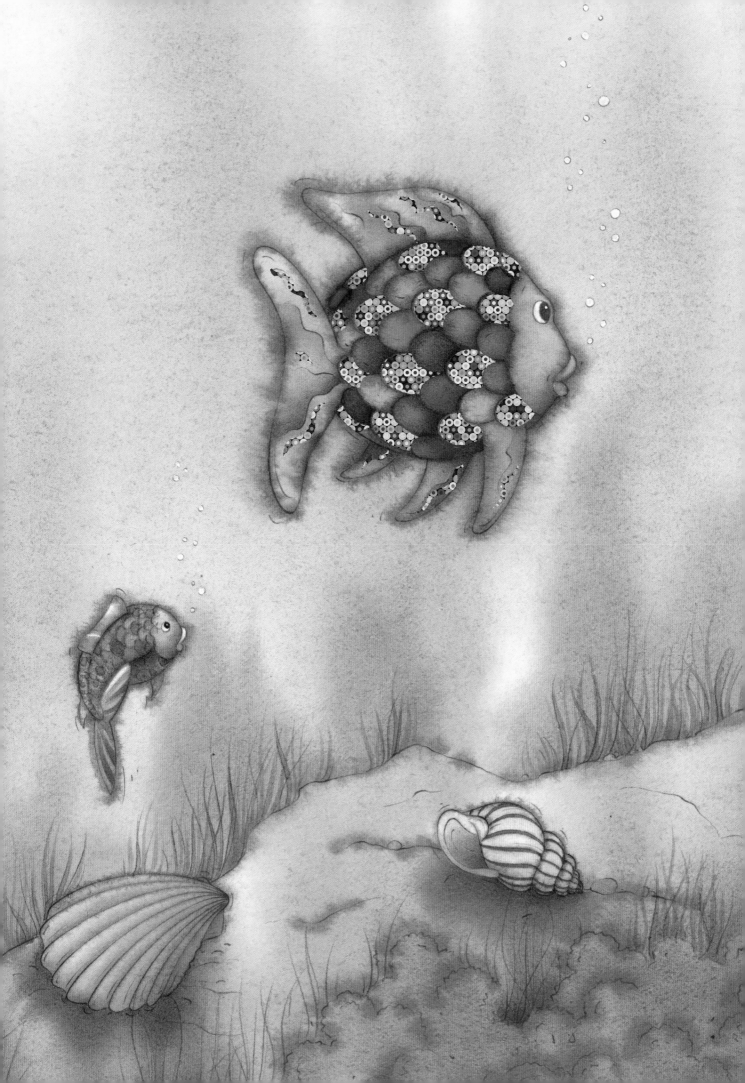

A little blue fish swam along behind him. "Rainbow Fish, Rainbow Fish, wait for me! Won't you give me one of your glitter-scales? They are so beautiful and you have so many!"

Un pececito azul nadó tras él. "Pez Arcoíris, pez Arcoíris, ¡espérame! ¿Por qué no me das una de tus escamas brillantes? ¡Son preciosas! Y como tú tienes tantas...".

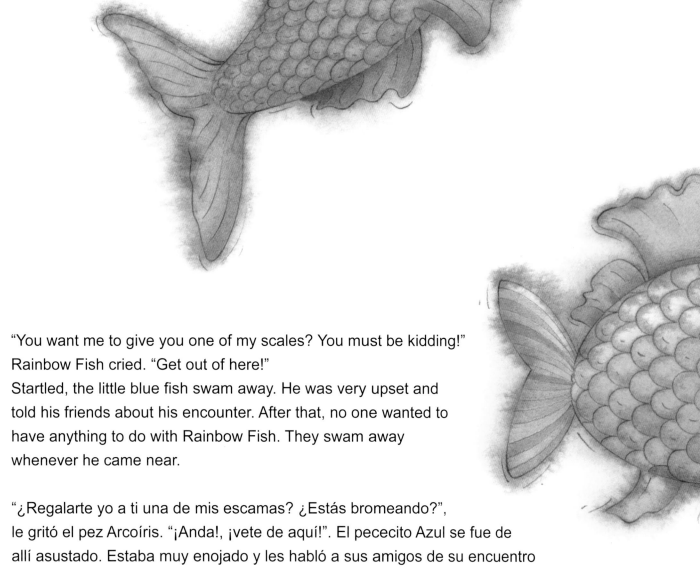

"You want me to give you one of my scales? You must be kidding!"
Rainbow Fish cried. "Get out of here!"
Startled, the little blue fish swam away. He was very upset and
told his friends about his encounter. After that, no one wanted to
have anything to do with Rainbow Fish. They swam away
whenever he came near.

"¿Regalarte yo a ti una de mis escamas? ¿Estás bromeando?",
le gritó el pez Arcoíris. "¡Anda!, ¡vete de aquí!". El pececito Azul se fue de
allí asustado. Estaba muy enojado y les habló a sus amigos de su encuentro
con el pez Arcoíris. Desde ese momento nadie quiso saber nada de él y le daban
la espalda cuando pasaba a su lado.

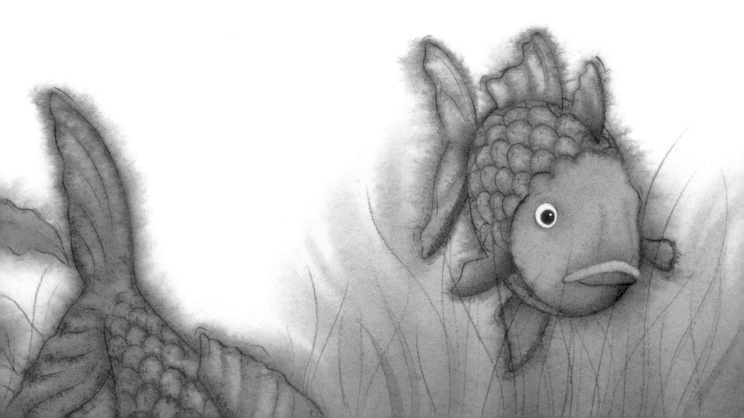

What good is it to have beautiful glitter-scales, when there's no one around to admire them? Rainbow Fish was now the loneliest fish in the whole ocean!

One day, he complained bitterly to the starfish. "I'm beautiful! So how come no one likes me?"

"The wise Octopus lives in a cave behind the coral reef. Maybe he can help you," the starfish suggested.

¿De qué le servían ahora sus magníficas escamas brillantes si no había nadie que las admirara? ¡Ahora el pez Arcoíris era el pez más solitario de todo el océano!

Un día fue a lamentarse a la estrella de mar. "Si soy tan hermoso, ¿por qué no me quiere nadie?".

"En una cueva detrás de los arrecifes de coral vive un pulpo muy sabio que se llama Octopus. A lo mejor él puede ayudarte", le aconsejó la estrella de mar.

Rainbow Fish found the cave. It was dark and a little frightening. He could hardly see anything. Then suddenly he saw two eyes shining back at him.

El pez Arcoíris encontró la cueva. Todo estaba oscuro y era un poco tenebroso. Casi no podía ver nada. Pero de repente descubrió dos ojos brillantes que lo miraban.

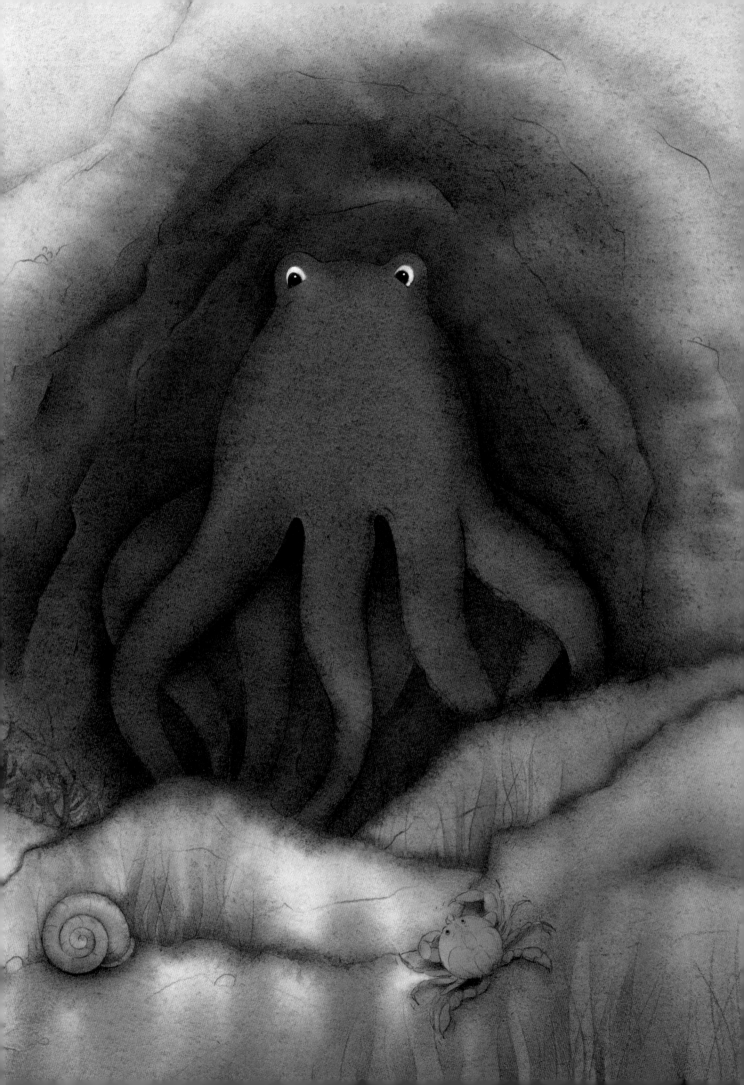

"I was expecting you," said Octopus in a deep voice. "The waves brought me your story. Listen to my advice: Give each fish one of your glitter-scales. Then you will no longer be the most beautiful fish in the sea, but you will be happy again."

"Estaba esperándote", dijo Octopus con voz profunda. "Las olas me contaron tu historia. Escucha mi consejo: regálale a cada pez una de tus escamas brillantes. Así dejarás de ser el pez más bello del océano, pero a cambio de eso volverás a ser feliz".

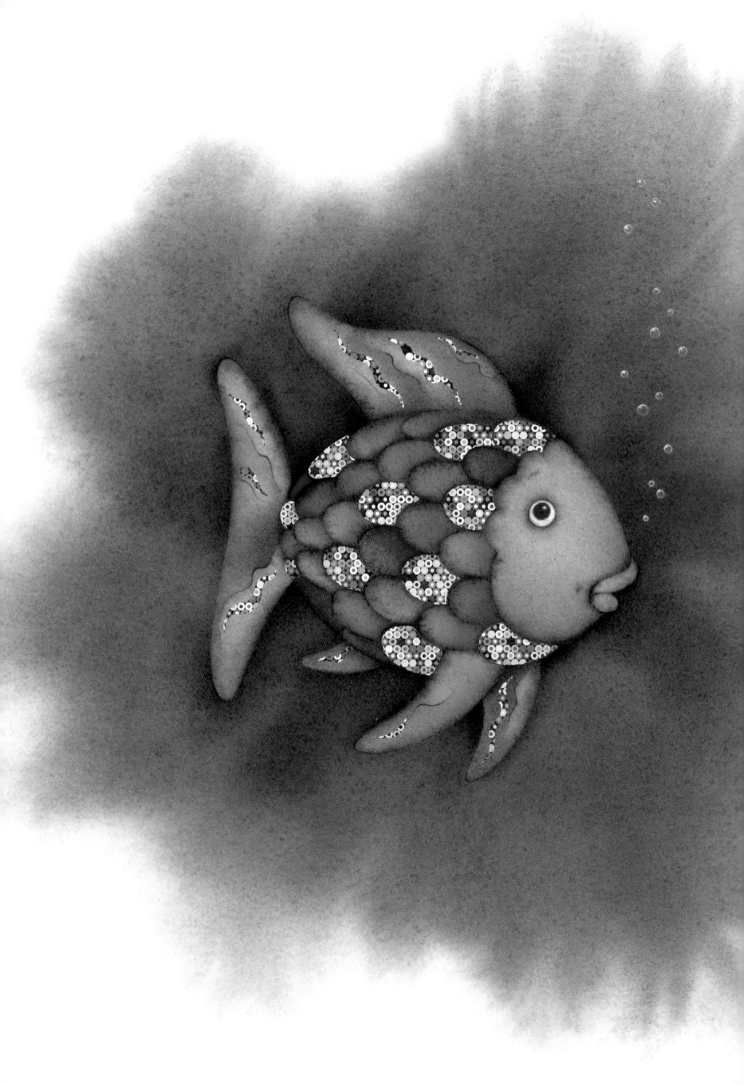

Before Rainbow Fish could object, Octopus had already
disappeared in a dark cloud of ink.
"Give away my scales? My pretty glitter-scales?" the Rainbow Fish
said appalled. "Never! No. How could I be happy without them?"

Antes de que el pez Arcoíris pudiera contestar, Octopus había
desaparecido en una oscura nube de tinta.
"¿Regalar yo mis escamas? ¿Mis bonitas escamas brillantes?",
dijo el pez Arcoíris horrorizado. "¡Jamás! No y no. ¿Cómo podría
ser feliz sin ellas?".

Just then he felt the light stroke of a fin nearby. The little blue fish had come back!

"Rainbow Fish, please, don't be angry. Won't you give me just one little glitter-scale?"

Rainbow Fish hesitated. "I guess I won't really miss just one teeny tiny little glitter-scale," he thought.

En ese momento notó junto a él un ligero aletazo. ¡El pececito Azul había vuelto!

"Pez Arcoíris, por favor, no te enojes. ¿No quieres darme una escama brillante pequeñita?".

El pez Arcoíris dudó un instante. "Supongo que no echaré de menos una escamita pequeña", pensó.

Carefully, Rainbow Fish plucked the smallest glitter-scale from his suit. "Here, you can have this one! But leave me alone now!"

"Thank you so much!" burbled the little blue fish with excitement. "You're so kind, Rainbow Fish."

Rainbow Fish suddenly felt very strange. For a long time, he watched the little blue fish joyfully swim away, back and forth through the water, carrying the glitter-scale.

Con mucho cuidado se arrancó de su traje la escama brillante más pequeña de todas. "Mira, aquí tienes, ¡te doy ésta! ¡Pero ahora déjame en paz!".

"¡Muchísimas gracias!", contestó el pececito Azul loco de alegría. "¡Qué bueno eres, pez Arcoíris!".

De repente, el pez Arcoíris se sintió muy extraño. Se quedó mirando un buen rato al pececito Azul, que nadaba en el agua de un lado para otro, feliz con su escama brillante.

The little blue fish darted through the water with his glitter-scale. It didn't last long before Rainbow Fish was surrounded by other fish. Everyone wanted a glitter-scale. And what do you know? Rainbow Fish started handing out his scales, one after the other. And he was feeling happier with each gift. The more sparkly the water became, the more he enjoyed being among the fish.

El pececito Azul se deslizaba por el agua a toda velocidad con su escama brillante. No pasó mucho tiempo hasta que otros peces rodearan al pez Arcoíris. Todos querían una escama brillante. Y, para sorpresa de todos, el pez Arcoíris repartió sus escamas una detrás de otra. Y cada vez se sentía más feliz con cada regalo. Cuanto más relucían en el agua, más disfrutaba él entre los otros peces.

In the end, Rainbow Fish had only one single glitter-scale left. He had given all the others away! And he was happy! Happier than he'd ever been!
"Come, Rainbow Fish! Come and play with us!" the others called out.
"I'm coming!" Rainbow Fish replied and off he went with the other fish.

Al final solo le quedó una única escama brillante. ¡Había regalado todas las demás! Y era feliz, ¡más feliz que nunca!
"¡Ven, pez Arcoíris! ¡Ven y juega con nosotros!", exclamaron los demás.
"¡Ya voy!", respondió el pez Arcoíris y se fue con los peces muy feliz.

NorthSouth Books and Edition bi:libri are proud to present a new line of multilingual children's books.

Launching with ten bilingual editions of The Rainbow Fish, this series will continue with further titles that address universal themes such as friendship, tolerance, and finding courage—bringing great stories and second-language learning fun to children around the world.

The following bilingual editions are available:

English/German
ISBN: 978-0-7358-4368-4

English/French
ISBN: 978-0-7358-4369-1

English/Italian
ISBN: 978-0-7358-4370-7

English/Spanish
ISBN: 978-0-7358-4371-4

English/Arabic
ISBN: 978-0-7358-4372-1

English/Chinese
ISBN: 978-0-7358-4373-8

English/Korean
ISBN: 978-0-7358-4374-5

English/Japanese
ISBN: 978-0-7358-4375-2

English/Russian
ISBN: 978-0-7358-4376-9

English/Vietnamese
ISBN: 978-0-7358-4377-6

Edition bi:libri is a publishing house based in Germany, specializing in bilingual children's books. Publisher Dr. Kristy Koth is American and did undergraduate studies in languages and second-language acquisition before completing an MA and a PhD in French Literature. She taught French in the US and English in Japan, France, and Germany before beginning her career in publishing, where she combines her knowledge about language learning with her passion for Children's literature.